THE HOUSE IN THE TREE

THE HOUSE
IN THE TREE

A Story of Israel

BY *Molly Cone*

Illustrated by Symeon Shimin

THOMAS Y. CROWELL COMPANY, NEW YORK

1 2 3 4 5 6 7 8 9 10

85   4-21-68   SSG   375/300

THE HOUSE IN THE TREE

In his aunt's house, everybody talked at once. Everybody asked questions, and everybody answered. Everybody but Yaacov.

He sat and stared out into the thick green branches of an olive tree.

Here everybody called him *Yaacov* instead of Jacob. Even his father and mother called him Yaacov since they had come to Israel. It was the way to say his name in Hebrew.

"Yaacov!" said his father. "Listen!"

"Just like his grandfather!" said Yaacov's mother. "Sits without ears!"

Yaacov turned his head to listen. But what he listened to was the whispering of the olive leaves.

1

"For Yaacov, everything is new," said his aunt.

His older cousin Izik grinned at him. Izik was a *sabra*. All children born in Israel were called sabras after the cactus plant that grew everywhere in the land. The cactus fruit was tough and prickly on the outside. But the inside tasted sweet.

Half of everything that was Izik's was now Yaacov's. Half his table, half his cupboard, half his bed. Half this house would be Yaacov's house all the year his family stayed in Israel.

"In America, Yaacov learned to say all the prayers in Hebrew," said Yaacov's mother proudly.

"But you have to live in Israel to learn what the words really mean," said his aunt softly.

Yaacov gazed at the olive tree. He saw thick wide limbs and a place for a floor. He saw a green-branched ceiling and space for a door.

"I think I will build a tree house," he said.

"A house in a tree?" His aunt seemed surprised.

Yaacov nodded. That's what he meant. A house in a tree. Like the one he had left in the empty lot back home.

Everybody laughed. Izik's was the loudest. But Yaacov saw nothing to laugh about.

"In that tree," he said.

They all looked at the tree. It stood outside their house of stone. It was an old tree. It might have been the same tree King David once sat under, it was so old.

In Israel many things were very old—as old as the land, the rocks, and the hills. And many things were very new—as new as the farms, the forests, and the flag.

The same land was called Judea long long ago. The people who lived there were called Jews, after their land. And their religion was called Judaism. They were the Children of Israel told about in early Bible stories.

Israel today is part of that very old land; but it is a very new country.

In that long ago time, other kings came into Judea and ruled over the Jews, and grew stronger and took their land away. Almost two thousand years went by before the Jewish people got their land back again.

"It is a land of miracles!" Izik's mother was always saying. As if miracles still grew from the ancient ground like the olive trees.

"You've got to have *wood* to build a house in a tree," Izik said.

"I'll find some," said Yaacov.

Their laughter followed him across the stony yard, past the low wall down the bare road.

"Don't go far!" his mother called after him.

4

He went past the store where his aunt bought dried peas and sesame seeds and orange drink.

He went past the stand where Izik and his friends bought *felafel* and *pita*. The pita was round and flat and looked like a pancake. Inside was the spicy hot ball of mashed chickpeas called a felafel. An Israeli ate felafel and pita almost as often as an American ate a hamburger in a bun.

Yaacov went past the school where his mother went every day to learn Hebrew.

"Shalom!" his mother had learned to say there.

People in Israel said "shalom" for "hello" and "shalom" for "good-bye." Shalom meant peace.

7

"L'hittraot!" Yaacov's mother had learned to say for "See you later!"

Everybody in Israel spoke Hebrew. They said shalom and l'hittraot like the people of the Bible four thousand years before. Like Abraham who lived in this land long ago. Like Isaac and Jacob.

During the long while the Jewish people had no country of their own, they hardly spoke Hebrew at all. They lived in different countries and began to speak other languages. All the time, they used Hebrew only when reading their prayer books. Most Jews who came to the new Israel to live had to learn to speak their old language once more.

"Shalom!" the woman in the bakery shop called out, smiling at Yaacov.

"Shalom," said Yaacov. "Do you know where I can find some wood?"

She shook her head and gave him a piece of honey cake.

"Everybody says my honey cake tastes like manna from heaven!" she said.

9

Yaacov tasted. It tasted just like honey cake to him.

"Todah rabah," he said for "Thank you" and went on down the street.

He stopped at the corner. Newspapers were hung like wash over a line. They were printed in different languages. They came from many different countries, as the people in Israel did. Most people had come since Israel became a state in 1948.

"Shalom," said Yaacov to the man sitting under the line of newspapers. "Do you know where I can find some wood?"

The newsman shook his head. He wore a little cap as some Jews everywhere do.

A lady was buying a newspaper. She smiled at Yaacov. "When we first came to Israel we brought all our furniture packed in a big wooden box. But when we got off the boat at Haifa there was no house ready for us to move into. So we took all our furniture out and lived in the box for a while ourselves."

She laughed very loud.

"A box?" Yaacov said.

"No one has to live in boxes any more," she said. "Anyone who has such a box saves it for the *Succot* holiday. The children decorate it with fruits and leaves. They sit inside to eat their meals like Moses and the wanderers in the desert."

"You look and maybe you'll find," the newsman said. "Even though it's still not so easy to find wood in Israel."

A young man had stopped to listen. He bought a paper too. "You mean it's still *impossible!*"

The old newsman wagged his chin angrily.

"Live in Israel as long as I have and you

won't say anything is impossible! Swamps turn into green valleys. Orange trees grow where only rocks grew before. And salt water is turned into fresh water. The impossible happens every day in Israel!"

Yaacov walked off. When he got to the next corner, he looked back. They were still waving their arms and shouting at each other.

A dog had run up and begun to bark at them. Two cats walking past stopped to meow.

No one was afraid to say what he thought in Israel.

Yaacov went on down the street. Someone passed him singing loudly. A woman came running out to meet an old man. He was carrying a bundle and a suitcase. The woman was crying and laughing at the same time. She made a lot of noise. But it didn't bother anybody.

Yaacov opened his mouth and tried to laugh the way Izik did. It didn't come out the same. He guessed it was because he didn't feel much like laughing. Yaacov wondered what it was that made people in Israel feel like laughing so much of the time.

Slowly he walked to the end of the street. He turned onto the main road. Israel was a very small country. If he followed this road in a bus or a car he could go from one end of the country to the other in a very short time.

Going one way, he would reach green hills with orange trees and cotton fields and farms and banana orchards. Going the other he would find desert and goats and camels and rocks of salt. Or he could follow the road through the hills up to Jerusalem.

He walked along a little way. He looked from one side to the other. He saw stones. Many stones. But not much else.

An Arab came riding along on a donkey. His long coat flapped below his knees. A white scarf, called a *kafia*, was wrapped around his head. Many Arabs live in Israel. Arab countries are Israel's neighbors.

14

"Shalom!" called Yaacov. "Do you know where I can find some wood?"

Salaam, said the arab. He shook his head and the donkey flicked his tail.

A bus came around the bend of the hill. On its side was D A N.

"Do you know where I can find some wood?" Yaacov shouted as the bus went slowly by.

But the driver only waved his hand.

Two soldier girls came walking by. Yaacov ran along beside them.

"Do you know where I can find some wood?"

One girl shrugged, pushed out her lip, and turned the palms of her hands up.

"I know where there's plenty of wood," the other said.

"Where?" shouted Yaacov.

"Over there." She waved toward the hill-top. "We just planted a whole forest up there!"

Yaacov looked at the new forest on the hillside. The tallest tree was as high as his knee. He watched the soldier girls out of sight.

A young man came riding along on a tractor. He wore shorts and sandals. A round faded hat was tipped over his eyes, *kibbutz-style.*

A farm that was a kibbutz was a very special kind of farm in Israel. Many many families lived together on each kibbutz like one large family. Everyone shared the work to be done. Everything on the kibbutz belonged to everybody equally. Kibbutz farmers were very important to the little country of Israel. They were making the old land new again.

"Wood?" the man yelled down. "It's against the law to cut down a tree in Israel! Nothing much of anything grew here until we came and planted. Nothing but rocks!"

Yaacov stood at the side of the road and watched the tractor disappear.

A small dusty car stopped. The driver stuck his head out the window.

"Is this the way to Jerusalem?" the driver asked.

Yaacov pointed to a sign. It said Jerusalem in Hebrew.

"I told you it was the right road," the woman in the car said crossly. But she smiled at Yaacov. The man took out his map.

"We've just come from Beersheba," the woman said, and added importantly, "where Abraham lived."

Yaacov nodded. Israeli children learned about Abraham and Moses, King Solomon and David, the way American children learned about Christopher Columbus, George Washington, and Abraham Lincoln.

Israeli children often climbed the mountain where David hid from King Saul. They visited King Solomon's mines or stood on the shore where Jonah set out in a ship and was swallowed by a whale. Many of the things told about in the Bible happened in this same land of Israel long ago.

The man put away his map.

"Did you see any wood I can use to make a house in a tree?" Yaacov asked them hurriedly.

The woman laughed.

"I've seen tents of goatskins, houses of stone and cement, and even huts of reed, but I can't say I've seen a house of wood in Israel."

Yaacov looked after the dusty back end of the car moving away.

A truckload of boys and girls roared along. The children sat on benches inside the truck and called "Shalom! Shalom!" at Yaacov.

Yaacov stood there without waving back.

He closed his eyes, saw the house in the tree with the leaves curtaining the window. Saw the floor of wood and the green-branched ceiling. He felt the sun smiling hotly on his head and he thought he heard the stones laugh. He opened his eyes.

A big black taxi had stopped in the middle of the road. The driver got out, opened the hood, and looked in.

A cloud of steam blew out. The man jumped back and laughed.

"Do you think I can find some wood anywhere around here?"

"Why not?" said the taxi man. "They say miracles happen every day in Israel."

Yaacov blinked.

"Ask anyone. Everyone has a miracle to tell you. It's a miracle we Jews are here!"

Yaacov watched him slam down the hood of his car and wipe his hands on a rag.

"Before I came to Israel, where did I live?"

"Where?" asked Yaacov.

"Nowhere," said the man who drove the

taxi. "In the country where I was born and where I grew up, there came a leader who said: *'Jews! This is not your home.'* And he took away my house and he took away all the things I loved. No place was my home anymore."

The man stood up straight and took a deep breath.

"In Israel no one can say to me: *'This is not your home.'* Here the people are Jewish and the ways are Jewish. In Israel even the land and the trees and the sky are Jewish!" He laughed very loud.

Yaacov stared at the sky. It was very high and blue.

"Two thousand years we waited and we dreamed. And finally we learned—'If you will it, it's no dream.' "

He winked at Yaacov. "Learning always takes time," he said. And he got back into his car.

"But I can't wait two thousand years!" Yaacov ran after him to shout.

An old man came by on a bicycle. Two long curls hung down over his ears.

"Stay out of the street!" he scolded, and shook his finger at Yaacov.

Slowly Yaacov went home.

Everybody was going home. In Israel, people closed the shops at noontime and went home to eat their dinners in the middle of the day.

In Israel everybody worked on Sunday and rested on Saturday. Saturday was the Sabbath for all of Israel just as it had always been for Jews everywhere.

That afternoon Yaacov looked again. He found a piece of an old clay jar and gave it to his father. He found a carob pod and gave it to his mother. He found three American gum wrappers. He kept them.

Many things may be found today in the ancient land of Israel. But Yaacov didn't find any wood.

After the evening meal, Yaacov got into his half of the bed. He dreamed of the tree house. He could see it there on the thick branch of the tree. He was still smiling when he opened his eyes in the morning.

"If you will it, it's no dream," the taxi driver had said.

Quickly Yaacov rolled out of bed. He leaned out the window and looked into the tree. But there was no tree house there.

"What's the matter?" said Izik, sitting up in his half of the bed.

"Nothing," Yaacov said.

"What's the matter?" said his father when Yaacov sat down at the breakfast table.

"Nothing," he said.

"What's the matter?" said his mother when Yaacov didn't go out to play.

"In Israel, everyone has problems," his aunt said. "So why shouldn't Yaacov have one too? If you didn't have problems, you wouldn't have miracles!" She smiled at Yaacov. "So now you are a real Israeli."

Yaacov tried to laugh. He didn't believe in miracles.

He helped the bakery woman wash her windows. But she paid him only in honey cakes.

He helped his aunt with the marketing. She gave him an apple.

33

"TEMPLE ISRAEL"

He helped Izik weed the carrots. "*Todah rabah*," said Izik. Half of Izik's chores were Yaacov's too.

"In Israel everybody helps," his aunt said. "Everything counts."

She held up an apple. "From the inside we make sauce or juice. From the outside, jam."

"You could make your tree house out of an old blanket," his mother said.

Yaacov shook his head.

"You could use rope to make a hammock," said his father.

"Or weave reeds into a basket like the one that held the baby Moses," his aunt said.

"You have to have wood to build a house in a tree," Yaacov said.

And no one laughed.

Izik said loudly. "We have more work to do! We have to go to the Post Office today."

Yaacov went to the Post Office to help Izik. He stood around while Izik filled out slips. He stared at the people going in and out.

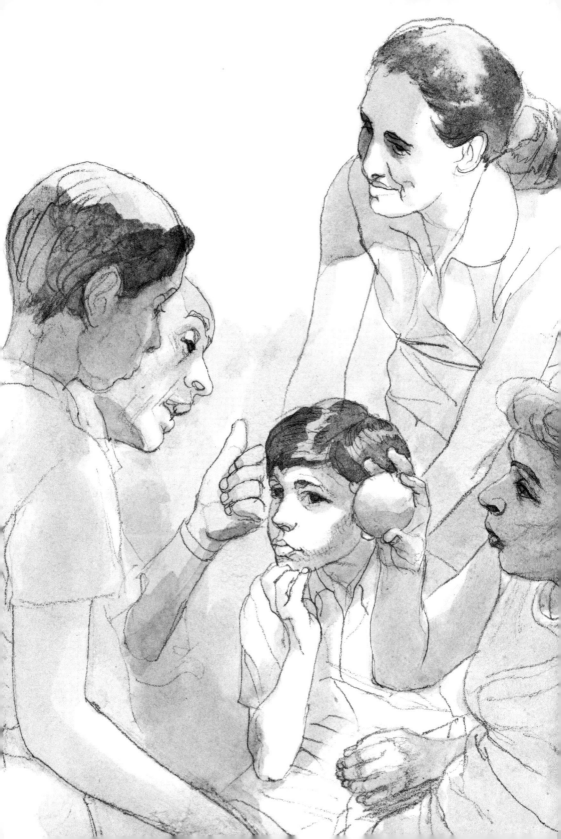

Some were very dark skinned and some very light. They were from many of the nations in the world. Some had come to Israel because there was no other place for them to go. Some only because they wanted to. They were Jews—like Abraham.

Like Yaacov.

If you will it, it's no dream.

"Here it is!" Izik said.

Yaacov turned around.

Izik was standing next to something. It was very large.

"Books," said Izik.

Yaacov opened his eyes wide. "Wood!" he cried.

"Oh," said Izik. Then he opened his mouth and closed it again. He put his hand on the box.

"It's half yours," he said carefully.

Yaacov held his breath. "Which half?"

"The books inside are mine," Izik said.

Yaacov looked at the crate and saw the house in the tree. He saw a floor of boards—wide as a floor should be.

"And the wood outside is mine!"

38

Izik grinned at him. "When you live in Israel, you have to believe in miracles," he said.

Yaacov laughed. Loud as you please. The way all Israelis laugh. "I know it," he said.

ABOUT THE AUTHOR

Molly Cone is the author of three Crowell Holiday Books, *The Jewish New Year, The Jewish Sabbath,* and *Purim. The House in the Tree* was written after a long visit in Israel, and reveals her delight in the people and their land. She is the author of more than a dozen other books for young and teen-age readers.

Mrs. Cone grew up in "a smallish city in the great Northwest where every family had a house, every house had a yard, and every yard had a dog." Her writing reflects the warmth and humor of family life. She and her husband and children live in Seattle, Washington.

ABOUT THE ARTIST

Symeon Shimin was born in Astrakhan, on the Caspian Sea, in Russia, and came to the United States with his family ten years later. He attended art classes at Cooper Union in the evenings. Mr. Shimin painted for a while in the studio of George Luks, but he is primarily self-taught and found his schooling for the most part in the museums and art galleries in this country and in France and Spain.

In 1938, Mr. Shimin was chosen to paint a mural in the Department of Justice Building in Washington, D. C. Recognition and many invitations to museum exhibitions followed, including those at the Whitney Museum of Art, the Art Institute of Chicago, the National Gallery in Washington, D.C., and the National Gallery in Ottawa, Canada. His paintings are in public and private collections.